This book belongs to

Magic in the Making

Published by Advance Publishers
www.advance-publishers.com

Written by Ronald Kidd
Illustrated by Kenny Yamada, Brad McMahon, and Yakovetic
Editorial development and management by Bumpy Slide Books
Illustrations produced by Disney Publishing Creative Development
Cover design by Deborah Boone

ISBN: 1-57973-028-0

The circus was in town, and everyone in The City
had a ticket. All the bugs in the audience were excited
as they piled in under the big top and took their seats.

P.T. Flea, the circus owner, stepped into the center ring. "Welcome to the World's Greatest Circus!" he cried. "Enjoy the show!"

First came the clowns. Heimlich played a bumble-bee. Slim and Francis were dressed as flowers.

P.T. Flea watched from the side of the circus ring. Much to his surprise, none of the performers was making any mistakes!

The following act was Dim, the giant beetle, and Rosie, his tamer.

"Now?" whispered Dim. Rosie nodded, and Dim let out a ferocious roar. Smiling, Rosie scratched him under his chin.

Next Tuck and Roll got shot from a cannon and began bouncing off the walls—for real. When they came to a stop, they slapped each other's hands and raced off, chattering in a language no one knew.

"Wow!" thought P.T. Flea. "I can't believe we're actually putting on a good show!"

Just then, Manny, the magician, appeared in a puff of smoke. His wife and assistant, Gypsy, was at his side.

"I will begin by performing my world-famous 'flower-and-seed trick'!" Manny announced.

He put three flowers on a table. He placed a seed under one of them. Then he quickly moved the flowers around.

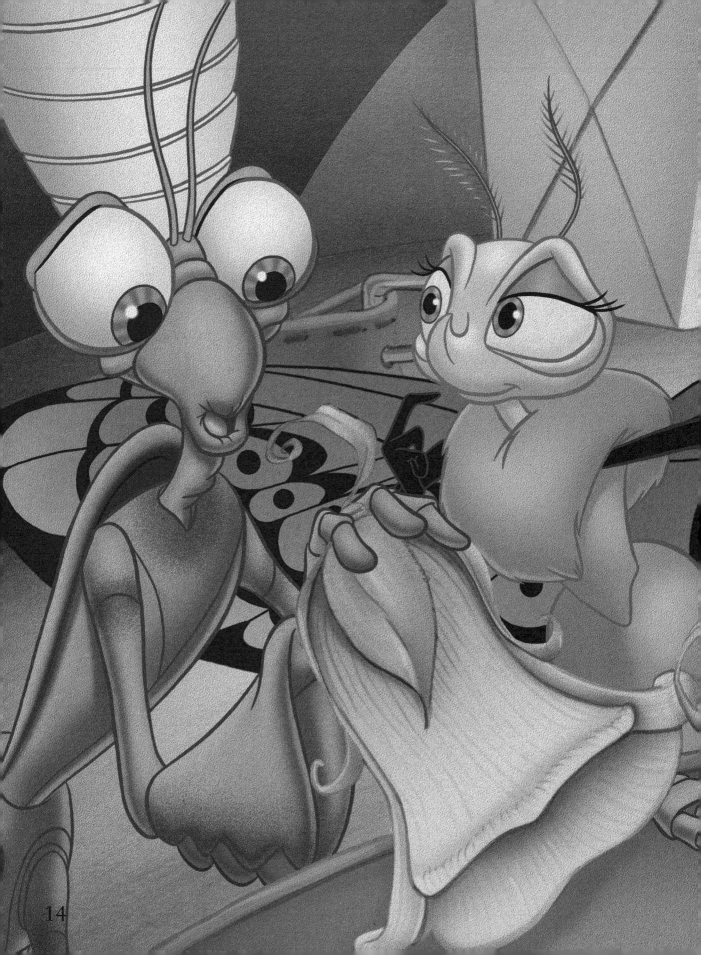

"Abracadabra!" Manny shouted.

But when he tried to find the seed under one of the flowers, it wasn't there. In fact, Manny couldn't find the seed anywhere.

"I knew it was too good to be true," P.T. Flea muttered to himself.

Luckily, Gypsy was ready. She spread her wings and quickly slipped a spare seed onto the table.

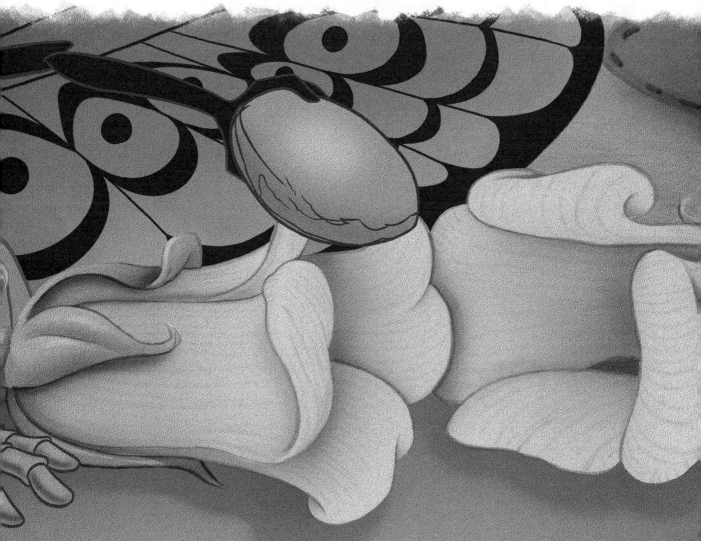

After the show, Gypsy seemed upset. Rosie told her, "I'm sure Manny will do better next time."

"It's not that," said Gypsy. "Tomorrow is our wedding anniversary. I don't think Manny remembered." Gypsy sighed. "He used to be so romantic."

Watching Gypsy leave the tent, Rosie had an idea.
She called the others together and told them her plan.

The next day, Francis went to find Manny and
Gypsy in their dressing room backstage.

"P.T. wants to see everyone in the big top right away!" Francis told them.

Manny and Gypsy followed Francis into the circus tent.

"Happy anniversary!" shouted Rosie and all their other friends.

"Oh, how wonderful!" cried Gypsy.

"What a surprise!" said Manny.

"Oooh! Let's start the party!" shouted a hungry
Heimlich.

Rosie asked if Manny would tell the story of how he and Gypsy had met.

Smiling at his wife, Manny began his tale.

Manny explained that in those days he had been the star of another famous bug circus. One evening he was performing in the center ring when he sensed something unusual in the audience. He tried and tried but couldn't make out what it was.

Then finally he saw it—a pair of beautiful violet eyes looking back at him from the audience. It was love at first sight! Manny was barely able to finish his act.

When the lights came up, Manny watched the
lovely moth with the beautiful eyes. It was, of course,
Gypsy. As she turned to leave, he saw the magnificent
markings on her wings.

Enchanted, he followed her. But before he could introduce himself, something caught Gypsy's eye. It was a very bright light. Manny saw her move toward it, because moths love light.

Manny knew that besides being bright, that light was dangerous.

He had to do something to rescue poor Gypsy! Shielding his eyes from the light, he quickly flew from the shadows. Then he grabbed Gypsy and flew her to safety.

Sheltered in Manny's arms, and away from the light, Gypsy came to her senses.

"Thank you," Gypsy gasped. "You saved my life."

"Madam, it was my pleasure," Manny replied. Then he reached behind his back and magically produced a beautiful flower! "For you," he said to Gypsy.

As Gypsy took the flower from Manny, she looked
into his eyes.

At that moment, they both knew they would be together for a long time.

The next day, Gypsy began working as Manny's assistant. Her beauty, her charm, the markings on her wings—all were important parts of his act.

Whenever one of Manny's illusions went wrong,
Gypsy was always there to set it right.

They made quite a pair—both onstage and off.
Soon they were married.

When Manny finished his story, he took Gypsy's hand and kissed it tenderly.

Gypsy smiled back at her husband. "Thank you for saving my life, Manny."

"Gypsy, I hope we'll make magic together for many years to come," said Manny.

The others cheered.

Gypsy gazed up at Manny. "I'll always love you," she told him.

Grinning slyly, Manny turned to Gypsy. "My dear, I'll bet you think I forgot our anniversary."

He picked up a cape and twirled it mysteriously. Suddenly a flower appeared from out of nowhere!

Gypsy beamed with delight. "Even after all these years, you still have a few tricks up your sleeve!" she declared.

Dear Blueberry Journal,

Today I asked Gypsy why she's always busy at night when the rest of us are sleeping. She explained that most moths rest during the day and fly at night.

Because they fly at night, moths are used to the dark. But they really love bright light. When they see a light at night, they gather around it, trying to get as close as they can.

It reminds me of the way I snuggle up to Aphie on cold nights. Whether you're a moth or an ant, it feels good to be cozy!

Till next time,
Dot